PIRATE POLL

by SUSAN HILL

pictures by PRISCILLA LAMONT

PUFFIN BOOKS

In the summer there was a fête on the playing field near Jack and Polly's house.

BOWLING FOR the PIG

Roll a penny

There were games and donkey rides

STANDARD
LOAN

UNLESS RECALLED BY ANOTHER READER
THIS ITEM MAY BE BORROWED FOR
FOUR WEEKS

To renew, telephone:
01243 816089 (Bishop Otter)
01243 816099 (Bognor Regis)

Gold doubloons

Pirate Hats

Cutlass

grenade

Anne Bonny
Blackbeard
Callico Jack

Pirate Names

"The Jolly Roger"
(Pirate Flag)

Ships Rat

Things

Treasure Map

grappling
hook

cat-o-
nine tails

Pirate drinks

compass

pistol

Telescope

For Mrs Dow's class

and raffles

and cakes and teas
and candy floss.

There was a clown, too. He seemed to pop
up everywhere. First he came and shook
Jack's hand. Then he tried to give
Polly a balloon.
"It's only Anthony's daddy dressed
up, silly," said Jack.
But Polly wouldn't look.
"I like people to look like themselves,"
she said.

In one corner of the field
was a tent, where you could
have your face painted.
Some children came out
looking like cats.
Or gypsies.
Or skeletons.

A rag doll ran up to Polly. She had orange cheeks and
black spiky eyelashes and a bow at the front of her hair.
"Hello. It's me, silly," said Polly's friend Tina.
But Polly wouldn't look.
"I just want people to look like themselves,"
she said.

In the autumn it was Jack's birthday.
"I want a spooky party," Jack said,
"because it's Hallowe'en."
So he had one.

There was a spider cake

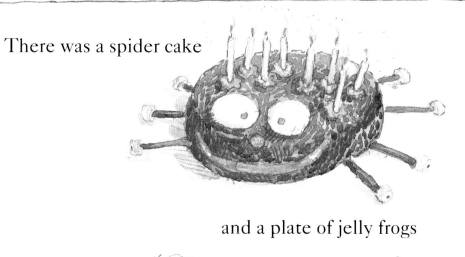

and a plate of jelly frogs

and the lemonade
was in a cauldron.

They borrowed the black cat Liquorice from next door,
and a lot of witches and wizards came.
They looked strange and scary.
Emma's hair was bright green under her pointed hat.
"It's only my friends, silly," said Jack.
But Polly wouldn't look.
"I just like people to look like themselves," she said.

In the winter there was a pantomime at Jack and Polly's school. The hall lights went out and some of the mums and dads and teachers came on stage to act the parts. The Wicked Fairy had a cackly voice and a scowly face and a dress that made her look fat. "It's only Miss Watson, silly," whispered Jack.

But Polly wouldn't look.

"I just want people to look like themselves," she said.

look out!

behind you!

That's your Dad isn't it?

In the spring, Mrs Jones said that next Friday
would be Pirates' day. They would have
pirates stories and games and sing special
pirate songs. Mr Gordon the caretaker
was building a pirate ship for the hall.
And all the older children
would dress up.

Jack dressed up. He wore Dad's belt with a
rubber dagger tucked into it. He had silver foil
buckles on his black gym shoes and a black
paper patch over one eye. Mum cut him a pirate's hat
out of cardboard.

And Grandma found an old knitted parrot
in a jumble sale.

He wore it perched on his shoulder.
"Yo-ho-ho! It's only me, silly," Jack said.
But Polly wouldn't look.
"I just want you to look like yourself," she said.
"You're just a baby!" answered Jack.
"Well, you were frightened of Father Christmas when
you were little." Mum said sternly, "I haven't
forgotten, even if you have."
Polly stared at Jack in amazement.
Jack went a bit pink.

When they got to school, there were lots of pirates.
Miss Watson and Mrs James and Mrs Lane were
pirates. Katie Richard's dad even drove his car to school
dressed as one. He had a big gold earring in one ear
and a huge hat, too.

Polly wouldn't look. She didn't even want to go into
school at all.
"I just want everything to be normal," she said.
But then Mrs Douglas took her hand.
"Come on, Polly. I think I know how to make you feel
better," she said.

Here's just the thing

In the little room behind the hall was the dressing-up cupboard. Mrs Douglas rummaged in it and found a stripy T-shirt, an old skirt with lots of coloured patches on, and a red spotted handkerchief. She helped Polly to put them on.

Then they found the face paints. And very carefully, Mrs Douglas painted Polly with a curly moustache and a black beard. The paint-stick tickled.

"Now," said Mrs Douglas, when she had finished. "Look in the mirror, Polly."

Just for a moment, Polly thought that she didn't want to. But then, she did look. And as soon as she looked, she began to smile. And after that, to laugh.

"Oh," she said. "It doesn't look like me. It isn't me. But it is."
"Yes," said Mrs Douglas, "I think we'll call you Pirate Poll.
Now - how do you feel?"
"Better," said Polly. "But I want to look like myself again later."
"So you will," said Mrs Douglas. "So will everybody.
That's the thing about dressing-up. How about having
this sword as well?"
"Hmm," said Polly. "Maybe."

In the corridor, they met Jack.
"Boo!" said Polly loudly.
Jack jumped.
"It's only me, silly!" said Polly.

Gold doubloons

Pirate Hats

Cutlass

grenade

Anne Bonny
Blackbeard
Callico Jack

Pirate Names

"The Jolly Roger"
(Pirate Flag)

Ships Rat

Things

Treasure Map

grappling hook

cat-o-nine tails

Pirate drinks

Compass

pistol

Telescope